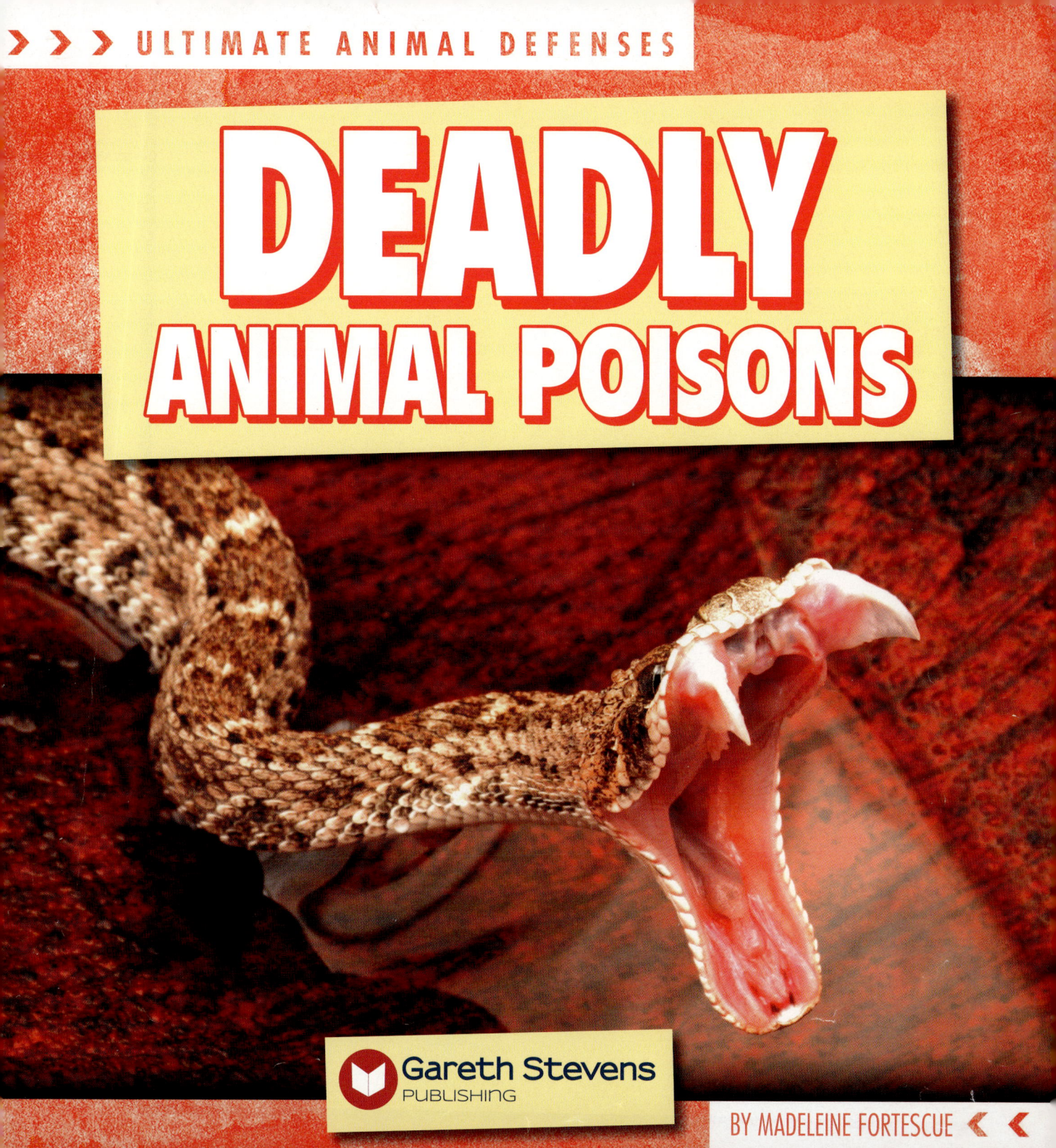

Please visit our website, www.garethstevens.com. For a free color catalog of all our high-quality books, call toll free 1-800-542-2595 or fax 1-877-542-2596.

Library of Congress Cataloging-in-Publication Data

Fortescue, Madeleine, author.
 Deadly animal poisons / Madeleine Fortescue.
    pages cm. — (Ultimate animal defenses)
 Includes bibliographical references and index.
ISBN 978-1-4824-4442-1 (pbk.)
ISBN 978-1-4824-4388-2 (6 pack)
ISBN 978-1-4824-4424-7 (library binding)
1. Poisonous animals—Juvenile literature. 2. Venom—Juvenile literature. 3. Animal defenses—Juvenile literature. I. Title.
 QL100.F625 2017
 591.6'5—dc23
                                            2015021482

First Edition

Published in 2017 by
Gareth Stevens Publishing
111 East 14th Street, Suite 349
New York, NY 10003

Copyright © 2017 Gareth Stevens Publishing

Designer: Katelyn E. Reynolds
Editor: Therese Shea

Photo credits: Cover, p. 1 Audrey SniderBell/Shutterstock.com; cover, pp. 1–24 (background texture) vector illustration/Shutterstock.com; p. 5 reptiles4all/Shutterstock.com; p. 7 enciktat/Shutterstock.com; p. 8 R. Gino Santa Maria/Shutterstock.com; p. 9 Jung Hsuan/Shutterstock.com; p. 11 Jason Edwards/National Geographic/Getty Images; p. 12 James van den Broek/Shutterstock.com; p. 13 Techuser/Wikipedia.org; p. 15 Auscape/UIG via Getty Images; p. 17 Berichard/Wikipedia.org; p. 19 YUSRAN ABDUL RAHMAN/Shutterstock.com; p. 20 warmer/Shutterstock.com; p. 21 (platypus) worldswildlifewonders/Shutterstock.com; p. 21 (millipede) Decha Thapanya/Shutterstock.com; p. 21 (Gila monster) Travelmages/Shutterstock.com; p. 21 (king cobra) CraigBurrows/Shutterstock.com; p. 21 (scorpion) Peter Bay/Shutterstock.com; p. 21 (stonefish) stephan kerkhofs/Shutterstock.com.

All rights reserved. No part of this book may be reproduced in any form without permission in writing from the publisher, except by a reviewer.

Printed in the United States of America

CPSIA compliance information: Batch #CS16GS: For further information contact Gareth Stevens, New York, New York at 1-800-542-2595.

CONTENTS

Don't Be Fooled! 4

Protected by Poison 6

A Fish's Poison 8

A Snake's Venom 10

A Spider's Venom 12

A Sea Snail's Venom 14

A Bird's Poison 16

An Octopus's Venom 18

A Primate's Poison 20

Glossary 22

For More Information 23

Index 24

Words in the glossary appear in **bold** type the first time they are used in the text.

DON'T BE FOOLED!

Some animals are just so cute you want to take them home to live with you. That's the case with some kinds of frogs. Certain small frogs in Central and South America are bright, beautiful colors, such as blue, red, orange, or yellow. But don't pick them up. These little creatures are poisonous! In fact, they're called poison frogs or poison dart frogs.

Poison dart frogs' poison is on their skin. The poison is dangerous enough that it can kill people if it gets into their body.

SO WILD!

All frogs have poison, but most aren't poisonous enough to affect people.

POISON DART FROGS' POISON PROBABLY COMES FROM THE BUGS THEY EAT. THE GOLDEN POISON DART FROG, SHOWN HERE, IS THOUGHT TO BE THE MOST POISONOUS.

PROTECTED BY POISON

Many kinds of animals produce poison. They don't make it just so they can hurt other animals. It's a way for them to **defend** themselves in the wild. Some animals don't have defenses such as large teeth or sharp claws. Poison and venom are **adaptations** that help these animals survive.

What's the difference between poison and venom? Poison can only hurt something if it's touched or eaten. Venom is poison that's injected, or forced, into a body by a bite or sting.

AN ANIMAL LIKE THIS DOESN'T NEED POISON OR VENOM TO DEFEND ITSELF. IT HAS OTHER DEADLY ADAPTATIONS!

A FISH'S POISON

Most species, or kinds, of pufferfish are found near Japan, China, and the Philippines. Many have rough or spiky skin to scare off predators, and many are poisonous. In fact, after the golden poison dart frog, the pufferfish is the most poisonous animal with a backbone on Earth. Its **organs** contain poison—as many of its predators find out.

Pufferfish are eaten in Japan. They must be prepared very carefully, though. A pufferfish's poison can stop a person's breathing. It's thought that one fish contains enough poison to kill 30 people!

SO WILD!

Box jellies of the Indian and the Pacific Oceans have 15 long **tentacles**. Each tentacle has 5,000 stinging cells that inject deadly venom!

> THERE ARE MORE THAN 90 SPECIES OF PUFFERFISH. THEY PUFF OUT THEIR BODY WITH AIR OR WATER TO LOOK BIGGER TO PREDATORS.

A SNAKE'S VENOM

You probably know there are venomous snakes. They inject their venom through teeth called fangs that have hollows or grooves. Many people think the inland taipan of Australia is the deadliest of all. It's reported that there's enough deadly venom in this snake's bite to kill 100 adult men! The venom works in as fast as 45 minutes.

Inland taipans will only bite people if they're scared. Most people who have been bitten receive **antivenin** to save their life. However, the inland taipan's small prey, mostly **rodents** and birds, aren't as lucky.

SO WILD!
The inland taipan's venom can cause bleeding and stop breathing.

THERE ARE THREE KINDS OF TAIPANS, ALL VENOMOUS. THE INLAND TAIPAN, SHOWN HERE, CAN GROW TO BE 5.5 FEET (1.7 M) LONG.

A SPIDER'S VENOM

A few spiders are fighting for the title "deadliest." One is the Brazilian wandering spider, sometimes called the banana spider. Its painful venom affects a person's vision, heartbeat, stomach, and finally makes them stop breathing.

However, the spider doesn't usually inject enough venom to kill someone. In fact, only 10 deaths have been linked to Brazilian wandering spiders. Scientists think they save their venom to protect, or guard, themselves against their predators. Luckily, there's antivenin available for this spider's bite.

SO WILD!

The Sydney funnel web spider in Australia has venom that can make a person's lungs burst!

THE BRAZILIAN WANDERING SPIDER DOESN'T SPIN A WEB. INSTEAD, IT HUNTS WHILE WALKING ON THE GROUND. THIS SPIDER WARNS OFF PREDATORS BY RAISING ITS TWO FRONT LEGS.

A SEA SNAIL'S VENOM

Sea snails can seem gross, but are they scary? There are about 500 species of sea snails called cone snails. The geographic cone snail is the most dangerous. This snail can give off **chemicals** that make its prey calm. Then the cone snail injects its venom using a tooth that it pushes out with great force. Its venom is toxic enough to **paralyze** sea creatures instantly!

Still, some kinds of crabs hunt the geographic cone snail. They try to break the sea snail's shell before they can be poisoned.

SO WILD!
A geographic cone snail's venom is made up of hundreds of toxins! There's no antivenin for it.

> GEOGRAPHIC CONE SNAIL VENOM HAS BEEN BLAMED FOR SEVERAL HUMAN DEATHS. THIS CREATURE IS USUALLY FOUND IN WARM, SHALLOW WATERS, ESPECIALLY AROUND AUSTRALIA.

15

A BIRD'S POISON

Poisonous spiders and snakes don't seem that unusual, but what about a poisonous bird? The bird called the hooded pitohui (PIHT-oo-ee) has a toxin on its skin and feathers, especially on its chest, belly, and legs. It probably comes from the beetles the bird eats.

Pitohui poison keeps away **parasites**, such as lice, as well as predators, such as birds of prey. Hooded pitohui parents may place the toxin on their eggs and chicks for protection. Snakes sometimes throw up after eating them! In humans, this toxin causes sneezing, burning in the mouth and nose, and watery eyes.

HOODED PITOHUIS LIVE IN THE RAINFORESTS AND JUNGLES OF NEW GUINEA, AN ISLAND IN THE WESTERN PACIFIC OCEAN. SOME PEOPLE THERE EAT THEM!

SO WILD!

Hooded pitohuis give off a strong smell that might be a warning of their poisonous nature.

AN OCTOPUS'S VENOM

The blue-ringed octopus has earned its standing as having some of the scariest venom in the world. **Bacteria** in a blue-ringed octopus's body make its venom. There are at least 10 species of blue-ringed octopuses.

The greater blue-ringed octopus is small. Its body is usually less than 2 inches (5 cm) long, and its arms are less than 3 inches (7.6 cm) long. This creature has enough venom to kill 26 people in just minutes! The greater blue-ringed octopus is found in the warm waters of the western Pacific Ocean.

THE BLUE RINGS OF THIS OCTOPUS GROW BRIGHT WHEN IT THINKS IT'S IN DANGER.

SO WILD!

The greater blue-ringed octopus has two types of venom. One is for paralyzing its prey, mostly crabs. The other venom, even deadlier, is for protection against predators.

A PRIMATE'S POISON

The slow loris is one of the only **mammals** in the world with a toxic bite. This **primate** gives off poison behind its elbows. When it's scared, it licks these places, mixing the poison with its own spit. This creates a venomous bite. The slow loris also puts the poison on its young's fur to keep them safe from predators.

Venoms and poisons can be pretty scary—especially if you're the predator of these animals. And if you're not, remember to keep your distance!

Some people don't count the slow loris as venomous because its poison's source isn't located near its mouth.

MORE POISONS AND VENOMS

The male duck-billed platypus has a spur, or spike, on its back legs that injects venom.

A millipede can release poison through its skin.

The Gila monster has grooves in its teeth to direct venom into an animal's body.

PROTECTED BY POISON

The king cobra's venom can kill an elephant in 3 hours.

Scorpions use their stinger to inject venom.

The stonefish has 13 venomous stiff points on its back.

GLOSSARY

adaptation: a change in a type of animal that makes it better able to live in its surroundings

antivenin: something that works against the effects of a venom

bacteria: tiny creatures that can only be seen with a microscope

chemical: matter that can be mixed with other matter to cause changes

defend: to keep something safe

mammal: a warm-blooded animal that has a backbone and hair, breathes air, and feeds milk to its young

organ: a part inside an animal's body that performs a special function

paralyze: to make something lose the ability to move

parasite: a living thing that lives in, on, or with another living thing

primate: any animal from the group that includes humans, apes, and monkeys

rodent: a small, furry animal with large front teeth, such as a mouse or rat

tentacle: a long, thin body part that sticks out from an animal's head or mouth

FOR MORE INFORMATION

BOOKS

Johnson, Rebecca L. *When Lunch Fights Back: Wickedly Clever Animal Defenses.* Minneapolis, MN: Millbrook Press, 2015.

Mitchell, Susan K. *Animal Chemical Combat: Poisons, Smells, and Slime.* Berkeley Heights, NJ: Enslow Publishers, 2009.

Riehecky, Janet. *Poisons and Venom: Animal Weapons and Defenses.* Mankato, MN: Capstone Press, 2012.

WEBSITES

Poisonous and Venomous Animals
explorable.com/poisonous-and-venomous-animals
Read more about the deadly adaptations of poison and venom.

Venomous Snake Facts
www.sciencekids.co.nz/sciencefacts/animals/venomoussnakes.html
Discover some fun facts about venomous snakes.

Publisher's note to educators and parents: Our editors have carefully reviewed these websites to ensure that they are suitable for students. Many websites change frequently, however, and we cannot guarantee that a site's future contents will continue to meet our high standards of quality and educational value. Be advised that students should be closely supervised whenever they access the Internet.

INDEX

adaptations 6, 7
antivenin 10, 12, 14
bacteria 18
birds 10, 16
blue-ringed octopus 18, 19
box jellies 8
Brazilian wandering spider 12, 13
duck-billed platypus 21
frogs 4, 5, 8
geographic cone snail 14, 15
Gila monster 21
golden poison dart frog 5, 8
hooded pitohui 16, 17
inland taipan 10, 11

king cobra 21
mammal 20
millipede 21
poison 4, 5, 6, 7, 8, 16, 20, 21
poison dart frogs 4, 5, 8
primate 20
pufferfish 8, 9
scorpions 21
sea snails 14, 15
slow loris 20
snakes 10, 16
spiders 12, 13, 16
stonefish 21
Sydney funnel web spider 12
venom 6, 7, 8, 10, 11, 12, 14, 15, 18, 19, 20, 21